This book is dedicated to all the families at the day care center who supported and believed in me despite knowing little about this book. For that support, I write for you.

- Jordan

www.mascotbooks.com

Might-E

For more information, please contact:
Mascot Books
560 Herndon Parkway #120
Herndon, VA 20170
info@mascotbooks.com

Library of Congress Control Number: 2015912022

CPSIA Code: PRT1015A
ISBN-13: 978-1-63177-115-6

Printed in the United States

MIGHT-E!

Written by

Jordan J. Scavone

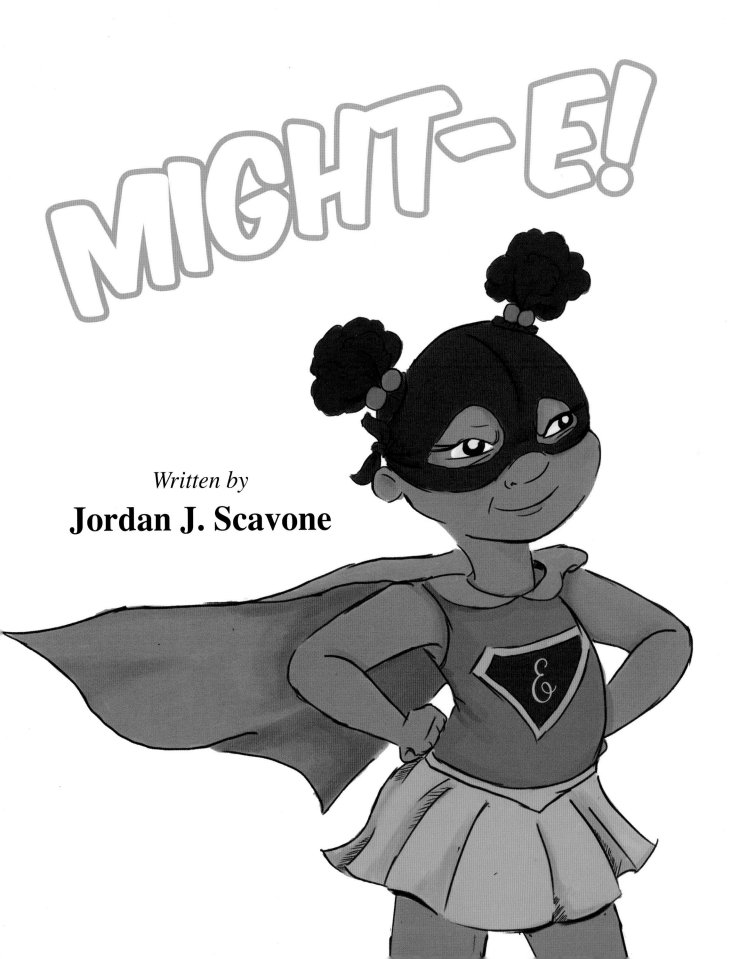

Some people are born to be heroes. They have that special quality, that one thing that lets them know they are destined to save the world.

Some can leap buildings in a single bound. Some are faster than trains. Some can even pick up an elephant right over their heads.

But, Emma was not one of those people. In fact when Emma was born, she was nervous, shy, scared, and would cry when anyone looked at her.

As Emma grew up, she became the shiest girl around. Nothing compared to the heroes she wished to be. Though she yearned to be brave, Emma just couldn't.

Emma's father thought, and thought, and thought, and finally he came up with a brilliant idea. "What a brilliant idea!" her father said.

On her fourth birthday, Emma's father gave her a gift: a big blue box, all tied up with a purple ribbon. Emma opened it, and inside was something that all true heroes needed.

A real superhero cape and mask! Purple of course, her favorite color. Now, when Emma would feel shy, or scared, or nervous, she would simply put on these magical garments and become...

MIGHT-E!

The bravest, strongest, and mightiest superhero the world has ever seen! However, despite being so mighty, her biggest challenge was just around the corner.

Now that she was four, it was time for Emma to start preschool. All her life she had dreaded that building. Going there would mean constant, daily interaction with other kids...without her dad! Despite secretly being Might-E, Emma did not want to go to school.

When the day came and Emma arrived at school, she stood in the doorway wanting nothing more than to climb back into her dad's truck. All she had was her purple (of course) backpack, and the hope her daddy would return at the end of the day.

Emma was greeted by five children in her class. Jenny was a redheaded girl with yellow bows in her hair. Jasper and Felix, were twins. The dark haired boy was Gregory, and finally there was Bree, a girl with a blonde ponytail on the side of her head. Emma was not feeling mighty.

Despite her fears, Emma did…kind of…well…just a little bit…like her teacher, Mrs. Madeline. Emma liked her because of her yellow dress with red polka dots. Emma liked that it looked like her purple (of course) dress with blue polka dots.

During morning snack, Emma sat quietly looking at her crackers. During playtime, Emma sat quietly holding her purple backpack tight. She didn't play with the other kids, she didn't even look at them. Emma felt less and less mighty as the day went on.

At naptime, once everyone else was asleep of course, Emma was able to calm down and finally close her eyes. Mrs. Madeline took the time to call Emma's dad. "I'm afraid Emma has been very shy today. She has not played with any of the other kids."

Emma's Dad laughed softly, "Check her backpack.
There's something that will help her feel more comfortable."

Emma woke up to find her backpack lying open. More fear rushed
over her…until…Mrs. Madeline walked over. Emma smiled and, with
Mrs. Madeline's help, Emma transformed into…

MIGHT-E!

And for the rest of the afternoon, the once shy and scared little girl was gone. In her place was the same girl, but now she felt comfortable being bold, brave, fierce, powerful, but most of all mighty.

Might-E was in such a good mood playing and protecting. Then, something happened. Her cape and mask flew off! They were stepped on and pushed aside. Emma was so busy saving the world and having fun, she didn't even realize it.

When Emma's dad arrived to see a joyful and playful Emma,
he was happy as could be. He scooped her up into his arms.
"Hello, my Emma!" her dad said.

"Dad! Shhh…I'm not Emma right now. I'm Might-E!"
Emma spoke with gusto.

"Oh, you are, are you?" Emma's dad turned to face a nearby mirror.

Emma was no longer Might-E, she was just Emma.
But Emma still felt like Might-E, even without
her costume. It was then Emma realized the other
kids were not that scary, and it didn't take a cape
or mask to be a hero. But...when things got extra
tough, Emma could still become...

MIGHT-E!

About the Author

Jordan J. Scavone created his first picture book at about six years old. This first book, written and drawn (well, stenciled), was titled *The Animals Look For Food*. It was about, well, animals looking for food. Though not the most well-thought-out (or well written) book of all time, this did plant seeds for the future. After receiving his undergraduate degree in Children's Literature and Theater for the Young from Eastern Michigan University, Jordan began working on his first picture book, the book you know hold. Neat huh?

Have a book idea?

Contact us at:

Mascot Books

560 Herndon Parkway

Suite 120

Herndon, VA

info@mascotbooks.com | www.mascotbooks.com